Table of Contents

Chapter 1

It's cold. It's February 4th and the wind is howling through the parking lot on South Virginia and Mt. Rose. The door at the Polo Lounge won't shut completely and every time someone comes in, Sam has to leave the bartenders mat to walk over and shut it. Hopefully, Manny will be in shortly to take care of that detail for him.

It's a Wednesday afternoon and the regulars start to arrive. The Polo has two kinds of customers; the afternoon crowd, as well as the Ricky B. fans and dancers who show up after 7pm.

A large man named Denny, a radio media type, shows up a little before five and starts a conversation of idle talk. Sam pours him a vodka rocks. Sam notices that for the past couple of weeks, Denny has looked stressed out and tired. He doesn't like to talk about his problems but Sam knows he has some financial woes. The recession has taken its toll on many of Sam's customers. Sam invites him to have dinner with him at seven o'clock at the Portofino, across the parking lot.

Manny shows up at 5:15pm, as always to take his usual seat at the corner of the bar. Sam senses his arrival and has a chilled bottle of Heinekens ready for him at his reserved station. It's not really reserved in the common sense, but everyone knows that that's Manny's seat. It's been Manny's seat for eight years, ever since Sam opened the place. Manny has his own reserved parking space in the back of the lounge, by the dumpster, and always enters and exits through the rear door.

Denny finishes his drink, leaves and says "I'll see you at the Portofino at seven."

The Polo, in Reno, is the most popular bar and cabaret in town. It draws quite a variety of people of every age group. It's a great meeting place for lawyers and the media. The young, twenty-five to forty-five crowd mixes with the more senior crowd that Ricky B. draws. Everyone seems to get along and enjoy each other.

Manny belts down his first beer and Sam puts another one down in front of him. In walks Neil, who like Manny has his own stool at the very end of the bar, by the cocktail server's station. Naturally, the door stays partly ajar and Manny knows it's his duty to once again shut it tight. It's not that he's obligated; he does it because the Polo is his home away from home and he just feels he should do it.

In walks Paddy, a short Irish carpenter who is the most opinionated customer Sam has. John also arrives about this time. Hank shows up and Sam walks over and starts a conversation. He's talking to Manny, Neil, Hank, John, and Paddy about politics. He knows a great bar owner's trick. He'll start a conversation and then walk away, leaving the customers to argue amongst themselves. He likes a lively bar. He hates silence. Paddy and John get into their usual tirade about the state of politics in the country. A very conservative Republican, John gets under Paddy's skin and they really go at it.

Leo shows up. Manny, always considerate of others, jumps up and gets Leo a special barstool, one without a back. Leo is a very large man and needs this stool. Manny takes the regular stool to where the backless one previously was and sits back down at own stool. Leo immediately feeds the electronic Keno machine twenty dollars.

Manny, in his earlier days, was a biker from Connecticut. He carries over a kind of macho/kick ass mindset from that time. However, at the same time, he's somewhat of an intellect and a great talker. He loves Rock and Roll and feeds the jukebox constantly. Being a former band member in a rock band, he also loves talking about guitar licks and rock music in general.

He's quite a character. While professing to be "ladies man," he swears and says "Fuck" in just about every sentence. However, no one seems to object. They accept him as he is. Everyone at the Polo has their idiosyncrasies; it's sort of a microcosm of life in general.

He is happy to tell you of his exploits with the biker world and relishes the opportunity to be the first line of defense of the Polo Lounge, should a fray erupt. Manny now works as a private investigator for a local defense attorney, Larry Dee. Larry has promised Sam that he would stop by, after work, this afternoon to talk about an upcoming private party that he wants to host at the Polo Lounge.

The Polo is actually comprised of two distinctly different areas. The bar side, where mostly local regulars hang out drinking, conversing, and playing the slots, is where the main entrance is. An archway in the wall allows one to enter the cabaret area, with its parquet dance floor, cocktail tables and stage. That room also has a front door that can only be opened from the inside. It is mainly used as a load-in door for the entertainers and musicians. However, some of the regular customers use is as an exit. Both sides have rear restrooms and doors to the alley out back.

Right above the stage is a mysterious area where Sam claims his office is. The general public is not allowed up there.

Sam, a great host and conversationalist, keeps the bar patrons happy. The customers love this guy. He is a tall, slender Italian man of seventy-six with snow white curly hair. Sam always dresses stylishly. A local newspaper columnist recently called him "The coolest guy in Reno." This is the thirteenth club he's owned. He started his career in the San Francisco bay area with several hopping joints. He hired the most famous rock groups to play his clubs and knows everyone in the business, as attested to by hundreds of pictures hanging on the walls of the Polo. Sam loves to show new customers these photos, most of them autographed by the famous celebrities, like Frank Sinatra and Tony Bennett. He absolutely charms people. Women drool over this man.

It's now about 5:30pm and the bar is full. Lisa, a very nice, widowed lady with a back problem, is at her accustomed seat, as well as retired doctor, Phil and his wife Cookie. Although a doctor, Phil leaves about every fifteen minutes to go outside and smoke. Two very attractive ladies are at the bar; Anna, a beautiful tall brunette, and Tamara, an elegant and foxy lady who does Elvira commercials. Manny, as usual is hitting on both of them. Everyone is having a great time!

About 5:35pm, Ricky B. walks in carrying his accordion and a bag full of miscellaneous wires and cords. He goes through the archway and enters the cabaret section. He likes to get there early to set up his keyboard and other gear. It usually takes a bout thirty minutes for him to set up.

He opens the front cabaret door from the inside and leaves it open so he can unload his heavier gear from his van parked in front. After the setup, Sam pours him a hot cup of freshly brewed coffee. Since he doesn't start until seven, Ricky sits at the bar and talks to Sam and the bar side customers while he waits for his loyal followers to show up.

Sam tends bar from opening until seven, when Cha Cha takes over. Cha Cha is a sexpot to the max. She has a great slim figure with black hair, large breasts and tattoos all over the place. She dresses very alluringly and the guys go nuts just looking at her. She also doubles as the cocktail waitress in the cabaret side.

At 7pm, Sam always leaves to go to one of the local eateries to have dinner. Sometimes, he'll take Manny and/or radio personality, Denny, with him, to keep him company. Between these guys, there is never a lull in the conversation. Tonight, he is going to the Portofino, a nice Italian restaurant right across the parking lot from the Polo Lounge. Manny decides to stay at the Polo, preferring to take his chances with the babes. That's okay, Denny will meet him there. He'll have company.

By now, the bar types that show up every day, to have their after-work cocktails, have left and now just the diehards, like Manny and the girls, remain. Paddy and John, who have called each other every conceivable rotten name in the book, are tired and have left. They'll go at it again tomorrow.

Ricky B. plays every Wednesday night from 7 to 10:30. He is a show-business veteran of many years and has the white hair to prove it. He plays the piano and accordion, sings and does his own unique brand of comedy. He does all kinds of music. His music really cannot be categorized because he loves jazz but also loves to play and sing Country. He keeps the comedy to a minimum at the Polo because the people come in to dance. He has learned not to mess with dancers.

Ricky started his Reno career in 1993 at a place called "Colombo's," similar to the Polo. He developed a following that has remained true to him to this day. He packs the place on Wednesdays.

Ricky is approaching seventy years of age but cannot retire for two reasons. First of all, he loves show business. He actually loves everything about it; the travel, the crowds, the energy, everything! He always shows up for work an hour and a half early just because he like being around the energy and the people. Secondly, he is broke and needs to make money desperately. In his life, he has managed to spend about two hundred thousand dollars more than he earned. He's not really depressed by this, however. He is an upbeat, Peter Pan sort of guy with eternal hope that one of his never ending business schemes will pay off, big time. His home, purchased several years ago, when times were better, is always under the threat of foreclosure. Tonight he's hoping to make fifty dollars in tips so he can cover a check that he wrote two days earlier. He has been a valued customer of loan sharks and various other street people over the period of his life.

The cabaret crowd slowly files in and takes their usual seats. The Polo patrons are territorial. Ivan and Sheila are usually the first couple to show, followed by Flo, a delightful, elegant lady in her eighties. Flo always sits up front, to the right of the stage. She has become the "Godmother" of the Polo Lounge. Everyone comes up to her and pays the proper respect. People love Flo. Always impeccably dressed, she is an amazing woman.

Ricky visits the men's room before starting. He doesn't take breaks as he has found that customers leave during band breaks. He'll be on stage for over three hours. The only time he ever takes a break is if another piano player drops by and sits in. Shelly B. is one of these. She is a pop singer and pianist who the Polo regulars have come to know and love.

He exits the men's room and signals Cha Cha to shut off the juke box. He heads for the stage. He scans the audience and it seems a little small; about a dozen people or so. He's not down because he knows, from experience; the place will be packed pretty soon. He never has a prepared set list, preferring to see what kind of audience he has and then picking tunes accordingly. Tonight he starts with a Bobby Darin classic, "Beyond the Sea." He'll ease into the night.

Within minutes, the place starts to fill up. Other entertainers drop by to sit in and sing a song or two. Tonight, Ricky is hoping Cleo, a jazz singer, and Paul; a Tony

Bennett Impersonator will show up to sing. Teri and her jazz saxophonist husband, Bruce, may stop by as well. Moe and his wife Carol will probably be coming in later. Moe is a very successful business man but a frustrated Jewish comic. Donny, A friend of Ricky's from the Colombo's days drops by with his wife, Judy. Donny is a Hawaiian with a nice crooning singing style. He always sings "Tiny Bubbles." A group of "Red Hatters" enter the mix. They all come over to Flo's table to pay their respects. All the regular dancers are now in attendance and the ladies change into their dancing shoes. It's a happening place and Ricky is thankful he still can earn money doing this sort of thing.

Sam has hit upon an entertainment formula that works. He uses Ricky on Wednesday nights and a Sinatra-like Frankie D. on Thursdays. Fridays and Saturdays are for the younger crowd with more rock and pop tunes played by a guy named Freddie, an old friend of Sam's. The place always does good business, thanks to Sam's great personality, his entertainers and bartending staff.

Meanwhile, Sam is sitting at the Portofino eating a salad, as he can't eat seafood or red meat. Denny, the radio guy, is talking about a promotion he thinks Sam should buy. Denny looks tired and Sam asks him how he feels. Other folks stop by the table to say hi. Everybody knows Sam and Denny.

Manny is still at the bar in the Polo Lounge flirting and laughing with Anna and Tamara. A few early twentyish folk come in and peek in the cabaret side to see what is happening. They see Ricky with his accordion and decide it's not their kind of place. They leave but are soon replaced by more of Ricky's following.

Sam finishes his salad, says goodbye to Denny, and tells him not to work so hard; get some rest. He then heads across the parking lot, back to the Polo to check on business. As a bar owner, he's always concerned about the head count and sales. He walks in to find most of the cabaret side full. He breathes a sigh of relief and starts socializing with the clientele.

Sam, because the ladies adore him, is asked to dance a slow song with one of them. Ever the gracious and accommodating host, he complies. After the dance he spots Manny at the bar and asks, "Have you seen Larry Dee?"

Chapter 2

"No," replies Manny. "The last time I saw him was at the office this afternoon. He told me he was going come to the Polo after he left the office." "Hmm; strange. I guess he got busy", says Sam. "I know he wants to talk to me about his party next month."

Manny takes his cell phone out and places a call to Larry. The call goes directly to voice mail, meaning the phone is powered off or Larry is talking with someone else. Manny says, "Larry, I'm at the Polo and Sam is wondering if you're coming down. I think he might be concerned that something is wrong. Call me."

An hour goes by with no return phone call from Larry. Sam says, "Something's wrong. He promised to stop by this afternoon and now it's after eight o'clock. He hasn't returned your call. This doesn't sound like Larry. Call his wife."

Manny dials Ruthie and she picks up. "Is Larry there?" "Why no, she replies. He told me he was going to the Polo Lounge after work." Not wanting to worry her, Manny says, "When you see him, have him call me."

The action in the cabaret side is really happening by now. Ricky is inviting guest singer after guest singer up on stage. The dance floor is packed and Ricky is on fire with his in-between tunes patter. His tip jar is filling up and all seems well. Cleo and Paul finally show up and the crowd goes crazy.

About 9:30pm Sam is about to leave for home and his wife. All of the sudden, what sounds like a gunshot rings out from the alley. Due to the stage noise, Ricky doesn't hear it and keeps on playing, wondering why everybody is running out back. Just about the entire entire audience; bar patrons included, are now outside in the dark alley. Finally, Ricky, left with no one to play to, goes outside himself.

Someone calls 911 and the police arrive. They look around with their flashlights and with guns drawn. Nothing seems unusual. Nobody's been shot and everything seems normal. No bodies in the dumpster or lying in the alley. What was the sound they heard that made them exit the Polo in such a hurry? Maybe it was just a car or truck backfiring. Everything calms down, the police leave and the people go back inside, thankful to get away from the wind and cold. Ricky returns to the stage and starts singing some Country tune with his black cowboy hat on.

Assuming everything is alright, Sam leaves for home. It's now about 10:15pm.

Ricky finishes the night at 10:30 and the party ends. He packs up his gear, opens the cabaret door, loads the stuff into his van and goes back inside to get paid by Cha Cha.   She says, "What a crazy night, huh?" Ricky says "yeah, I need a Stoli." Cha Cha pours him a good one on the rocks. He always has one cocktail at the end of the evening. It relaxes him after dealing with the demands of the customers during the night. He only has one drink, as he must drive ten miles to get home. He certainly doesn't want a DUI. He couldn't afford the fine, let alone the fee Larry Dee would charge him to represent him in court.

After spending about thirty minutes at the bar with Cha Cha and a couple of drunks, Ricky leaves for home, driving ever so carefully, not to attract attention by the cops. He gets home, changes into his nightclothes, turns on the the Letterman show, and pours himself another vodka.

Cha Cha stays at the Polo after everyone has gone and begins her cleanup routine. She picks up the glasses and table mess, loads the dishwasher and empties the trash into the dumpster out back. She also brings the tables and chairs that are outside the front door, for the smokers, inside and puts them on the dance floor. She locks the front and rear doors on both sides. By this time she is tired and needs to get off her feet.

She decides she needs a cocktail, herself, and decides to have it in Sam's upstairs loft where the couch is comfortable and she can stretch out, maybe watch a little TV. She knows that it is Sam's room but, what the hell; she cleans up there so why would he care?

She climbs the stairs. In the dim light, she turns on the TV and prepares to lie down on the couch. Still standing, she puts the glass to her mouth and sips on her drink. She sets the drink down on the coffee table and plops herself down on the couch. She screams, "Oh My God!" She has just landed on top of what feels like a body. She flips on the light and shrieks.   She has blood all over her clothes and skin.   She literally jumps down the stairs, knocking over lamps and her drink. Shaking like a leaf, she races outside and calls Sam, at home, on her cell phone.

Panicked, she stumbles through the words, "Sam, there's a man in your upstairs room at the Polo. I think he's dead!"

Chapter 3

"What? Say that again."

"There's a dead man upstairs in your office. I was upstairs after cleaning up and I accidentally sat on him. I didn't know he was there; it was dark. I've got blood all over me. I'm scared to death. What do I do?"

"Do you know who it is?"

"Not by name, but I've seen him in here before." She is trembling.

"I'll be right down. You call 911 and tell them to get over there, fast."

Sam jumps into his red Corvette and races the five or six miles to the Polo Lounge. He screeches into the parking lot and sees the place teeming with cops, fire trucks, and ambulances. He sees Cha Cha with a blanket over her shoulders, talking to someone, maybe a detective. It's now about two in the morning. Sam wonders why everyone is in the parking lot and not inside where it's warm?

Shortly, Jeanie, Sam's wife pulls into the parking lot, as well. Sam left in such a hurry that he didn't tell her what was going on. She got worried and followed him in the SUV.

The wind is now really blowing and it's down to around thirty-five degrees. It's extremely uncomfortable but the cops have to figure out what's going on. They don't want the crime scene contaminated. The body has no wallet or identification in the Navy blue suit pockets. Sam ignores the cops and runs inside, up the stairs, takes one look at the body and says, "Oh my God, It's Larry Dee! I don't believe it."

The cops know that name. Sam calls Manny at home. He's the only one who knows Larry's home number. He says, "Call Ruthie, something terrible has happened." Manny does as instructed and Ruthie comes tearing down, breaking speed limits, all the way. Manny also returns to the Polo.

Manny thinks, "Where's Larry's Lexus?" There is no sight of it in the parking lot.

A little history on Larry: Larry Dee is considered to be the leading defense attorney in Reno, Nevada. He and his wife are avid golfers and have been known to gamble large amounts of money at the local casinos. They believe in supporting the local economy, even in bad times. To everyone's knowledge, Larry doesn't have enemies. Although somewhat arrogant and egotistical, like most attorneys, he is generally conceived as a good guy, well liked, and admired. Who would possibly want to do harm to Larry? He has probably lost his share of cases in court but all attorneys face that fate, many times over, in their careers. No one had ever made a threat, to anyone's knowledge.

The coroner is called and, within minutes, determines the body has been dead for less than ten hours. The last time anyone spoke with Larry was about 4:30pm, and that was when Larry was leaving his law office. He told Manny he would probably see him at the Polo, as he needed to talk to Sam about a private party that he wanted to host.

The lead detective, A.J. Romero, decides that he must interview anyone who was at the Polo Lounge in the past eight to ten hours. Although it's now 2am, Romero doesn't care. This is going to make the morning news and he wants answers, now.

Romero works four ten hour shifts from 10pm until 8am. He has every Friday, Saturday, and Sunday off. He likes that, as he can spend time with his five year old grandson, Mario. He has two children by his ex-wife. Mario is his daughter Gina's boy. Although Romero and his "ex" battled for years, they seem to get along better these days.

He loves this job but has developed ulcers over the years. Still, he lives for the action. He's addicted to it. The short, slightly overweight, fifty-two year old Italian with the receding hairline starts instructing Sam and Manny to phone people. He asks for other's phone numbers and he makes some of the calls, himself

Ricky's phone rings at 2:10am and he groggily answers. He had been drinking vodka and he is pretty incoherent. He has only been to bed for two hours.

However, he has slept enough to hear the words "This is Reno detective A.J. Romero. You need to return to the Polo Lounge Immediately."

"Huh, he replies."

"Immediately," says Romero. As usual, Ricky is running low on fuel and must spend much of his tip money on gas. With exactly nineteen dollars in his pocket, he arrives at the Polo Lounge about thirty minutes later.

He sees Sam and Jeanie and asks what the hell is going on? Sam informs him that Larry Dee has been shot and is lying upstairs in his office. In disbelief, Ricky replies "What the fuck?"

Detective Romero comes over and introduces himself. "I'm detective Romero from RPD. I'd like to ask you a couple of questions."

Ricky is a pretty friendly guy but a little wary of cops, sometimes. "Are they suspecting me," he asks himself.

"Sure, ask me anything. I was here from 5:30 to 11pm."

"Exactly how do you know Larry Dee?"

"Well, I first met Larry years ago when I was playing at Colombo's, down on the river. We've been acquainted ever since through my gigs at various Reno clubs. I would see him and his wife, occasionally, at these gigs. They were always very nice and complimentary to me. We never really socialized with each other and I never had need for his professional services. I played golf with him on a couple of occasions." That's about it."

"Did he owe you money?"

"Hah, no one has ever owed me money. It's always been the other way around."

 "Have you ever been to his home?"

"No, I haven't had the honor of being invited."

"Do you own a gun?"

"No, I'm a liberal/independent. I am against guns, except for hunting in the need of food."

"Do you mind being fingerprinted?"

"Yes, I was fingerprinted at the Police Department years ago when I applied for a Gaming permit. You already have them."

"That's fine. Is there anything else you wish to tell me?

"No."

"Okay, here's my card. If anything comes to mind, please call me."

"You got it."

Chapter 4

Shortly, others start to arrive at the crime scene. The police have now allowed people inside, out of the cold. The cops are probably freezing, themselves.

The detectives are upstairs, taking fingerprints and processing the crime scene. Everyone else is downstairs, sitting at the cocktail tables in the cabaret side, waiting to be interviewed by A.J. Romero. It's now 3:30am, Thursday morning.

Everyone is asked when they arrived, what they heard, what they saw, when they left. There are about twenty people inside, including Cha Cha, Sam and his wife, Ruthie, Manny, and Ricky. Romero asks Ricky and Sam to call anyone that they know that were there that night. He wants to talk to them immediately.

Ricky gets on his cell and dials singers Paul and Cleo. They're both pissed that he woke them up. He explains the situation and they agree to come down. He also calls Flo and Shelly, the guest piano player. It is now almost four in the morning. Moe and Carol, Donny and Judy are called, as well as Bruce and Teri. Flo, being a Red Hatter, herself, calls the other Hatters that were in that night. Sam has phone numbers for some of the regular dancers that were there and he calls them too. He calls Denny, the radio guy, and leaves a message. Everyone is tired and cranky. Romero doesn't care. He works this shift normally. All he cares about are results and closing cases in a hurry.

Since he has already interviewed Ricky, he dismisses him. Ricky wants to stick around to find out what happened so he stays. Romero asks Sam what his past twelve hours have been like and Sam answers in pretty good detail, telling him about his early afternoon shift at the bar, his dinner at the Portofino with Denny the radio guy, coming back to the Polo to check on business, and leaving around 10:15pm. He is asked about the gunshot that everyone but Ricky heard. Sam tells him that he had the same reaction as everyone else; to run out back to find out what the hell was going on. He was asked if he went upstairs that afternoon or night. He said that he had not. He just uses that office to relax and frame pictures for the club. He has dozens of pictures in that room. His main office is downstairs at the far end of the bar. That is where the money is counted and put in a safe. He always comes by the next morning to take it to the bank.

All the customers tell Romero the same story. They were just minding their own business when the shot rang out. They all remember getting up and rushing outside to see what happened. They recall two police cars responding to a 911 call. They watched as the four officers combed the area, finding nothing. No body, no shells, nothing.

The other C.S.Is are wrapping up the scene and the body is carried downstairs in a body bag. It is placed in the waiting ambulance and whisked away.

Romero wraps up the initial interviews around 4:30am and sends most of the folks home. Before they leave, however, Romero asks them to call him if they suddenly remember any other details.

Ricky, Sam, Jeannie, and Manny remain. Ruthie, in a state of shock, is taken to the hospital in an ambulance, where she will remain under watch.

Romero wonders why the body was found without identification. Larry Dee, a prominent attorney, would surely be carrying ID. Also, he wonders why his cell phone can't be found. Larry always carried his iPhone. Also missing is Larry's Rolex, and of course, the Lexus.

The detective determines Larry was shot once in the chest, through the heart. It certainly doesn't appear to be a suicide. Why would he get rid of his ID if he was going to shoot himself? Besides, no gun was found. This looks like a genuine robbery-murder to him.

He questions the remaining few again. "Exactly, what time did you hear the gunshot? Where were you sitting?"

"Again, who are you, Manny, and why are you here?"

Manny replies, "Like I told you before, I work for Larry Dee as a private investigator. I have been with Larry for over twenty years. He's my best friend and confidant. I'm pretty shook up over this, as you might imagine."

"When was the last time you saw him?"

"Again, about 4:30pm, when he left the office. He told me he would probably see me here at the Polo later on."

"Did he seem upset, did he act strange?"

"Not really."

"Did he have his cell phone with him?"

"I don't really recall but I know it's always with him. He's attached to that phone"

"And what time, again, what time did you leave the office and when did you arrive here?'

"I always leave the office at five and get here at 5:15. I'm here six days a week. I park my pickup out back"

"Can you prove you were at the office until five?"

"Larry's secretary, Debbie can tell you I was. She'll be in the office in a few hours."

"Who has his credit card numbers?"

"Probably his wife, Ruthie, or his secretary, Debbie"

"I need those quickly."

"Well, as you know, Ruthie was taken to the hospital. I doubt if she can give them to you right now. Debbie will be in the office pretty soon."

"Why do you park out back?"

"To tell you the truth, I don't really know. I've always parked there. It's going on eight years now. Sam just lets me. I park right next to the green dumpster."

"Okay, since you are the last one to see and talk with the victim, I would like to talk with you more. I'm sure, as a P.I., you can understand."

"Of course," replies Manny. He writes his cell number down on a napkin and hands it to Detective Romero.

"And you, Cha Cha, you discovered the body. What exactly were you doing up there?"

"I just wanted to relax with a cocktail, kick back and watch as little TV. It's been kind of a stressful night."

"What made you go upstairs? Couldn't you have had your drink at the bar?"

"I usually do but I just wanted to chill out on the couch." I didn't think Sam would mind."

"Sam interrupts, "It's fine; she's a trusted employee. She's worked with me many years."

Romero asks, "Again, how did you discover the body?"

"I actually plopped down on it. In the dim light, I didn't see it on the couch."

Manny announces that he's leaving. He wants to be at the office when Debbie arrives to tell her of the bad news. He also wants to check on Ruthie in the hospital. Before he leaves, Romero asks him for Larry's cell number.

Romero still is questioning the remaining few people. "Does anyone have anything to share with me?"

By now, everyone is completely exhausted. Romero asks everyone for their phone numbers and dismisses the group. Sam locks up the place and goes home. Jeanie follows him in the SUV.

Chapter 5

It's now Thursday morning and everyone is watching the local news on TV.

"We have breaking news." Late last night, the body of local defense attorney, Larry Dee, was found shot in the Polo Lounge, on South Virginia Street. The body was discovered in an upstairs office by the night bartender, after her shift. We will update you on details as they come in. Again, attorney Larry Dee, was found shot to death at a local nightclub. Once we hear from detectives, we will update you on the situation. Please stay tuned for more on this"

Detective Romero is now home, after his shift. For some reason, he can't seem to go to sleep even though he has completed his paper work on his initial investigation and he's tired. He turns the news on and hears the same announcement that the rest of the city just heard. He has tried to call Larry Dee's cell number three or four times. Each time he is routed directly to voice mail. "Hello, you have reached the voice mail of Larry Dee. Please leave your message."

Sam's home phone rings. It is Channel 4, the NBC affiliate. They want to know everything.

"My wife and I are extremely overcome with grief at this moment. We don't know what happened or when. We are waiting to hear from the detectives. As soon as we know something, we will call a press conference. At this time, we don't know any more than you. To all our wonderful customers at the Polo Lounge, we will probably be closed for a few days. Our love and condolences go out to the family of our good friend and customer, Larry Dee. That's all I can say right now."

"Do you know of any suspects," they ask.

"No, and I certainly do not want to speculate. Like I said, we'll call a press conference once the detectives have some news. Goodbye."

Detective Romero finally fades off to sleep and wakes around 6pm. A Bachelor, he makes himself a salad and a tuna fish sandwich. He turns on the news and the Polo situation is all over the news. He calls police headquarters to ask of any new developments in the case while he was sleeping. "Yes, we've discovered a gun. I'll fill you in when you arrive." He tries Larry's cell phone again with the same result. He watches a few sitcoms, hits the shower and dresses for his nightly shift which starts at 10pm.

There are a few details that are nagging at him. Why was the body discovered upstairs? Cha Cha, the bartender said that, as far as she knew, no one was even up there. She heard no voices coming from that area all night. Sam, who worked a shift earlier, said the same thing. Why was there a dead body in an upstairs room? He didn't shoot himself. There was no gun or shells. There had to be a suspect who was up there with him, unbeknown to everyone. But then he remembers that the shot was heard outside. Why no ID or cell phone? This is a puzzler. Could it be a robbery that was set up by someone Larry knew?

With all the juke box noise in the afternoon, Romero decides it could have been possible for two or more people to go unnoticed, upstairs. Sam would never check it because he only goes up there in once in a while to fool around with his beloved photos. Could people sneak up there without being noticed? Whoever was up there had to walk past the bar. Cha Cha showed up about 6:30 to relieve Sam. She walked behind the bar to the office to say hi to Sam, who was doing some office work. Sam is always happy to see Cha Cha because that means he can leave and go eat with his buddies.

Perhaps some people came in while she was back in the office? There was about a minute or so with nobody behind the bar to see the room and what was going on. They were both in the office.

The cabaret side has a front door which can only be opened from the inside and a rear door that is never used but kept unlocked during business hours because of fire regulations. Could someone have entered through that rear door, out of sight of the bar area? Of course they could, he determines.

Because none of the bar patrons saw Larry enter, the only way he could've gotten in was through that rear door in the cabaret side. Someone must have been with him. Whoever shot him didn't carry him up the stairs. There was no blood on the stairway carpet or railing. The only blood was on Larry and Cha Cha and of course, the couch. Therefore, they must have entered together and walked up the stairs, out of sightline of the bar.

The lab tests wouldn't come back for a few days. The blood on Cha Cha was being tested for a match with the blood on Larry.   Fingerprints were being analyzed through the police database. Romero uses his seniority influence to hurry things up. He wants answers, now!

Who was up there with Larry Dee and why was Larry Dee up there in the first place?

Two things were certain. Manny, his trusted P.I. and his secretary, Debbie, were the last people known to have seen Larry. Cha Cha was the one who discovered the body. Everything else is up in the air.

Chapter 6

Meanwhile, about twelve hours earlier, in a casino in Wendover, Nevada, a middle aged couple is playing slots at the bar. They've stopped to refuel and get something to eat after a long drive from Reno. Even though they have a large sedan, the drive is still tiring.

They order breakfast at the bar and continue playing the slots. One could assume this couple to be comfortable with casinos. Ordinarily, people prefer to eat breakfast in a coffee shop. Only bar folk, meaning anyone who works in bars or casinos, are comfortable eating at a bar. They probably have worked in the business.

They finish their breakfast, drink another cup of coffee, and pay their tab with a credit card. Each one hits the restroom before another drive to Salt Lake City. Walt and Vanessa then exit the casino and head for the Lexus. It's now about five o'clock, Thursday morning.

Chapter 7

The detective calls Sam, Ricky, Manny, Secretary Debbie, and Cha Cha for another meeting at the Polo Lounge Thursday night. "I need to meet with you all at 10pm." Everyone agrees to meet.

Sam arrives first and unlocks the front door. He puts a pot of coffee on. This could be another long night. He is tired already from the media questions he's been getting, all day.

Soon the others arrive. Romero is meeting Debbie, Larry's secretary, for the first time. He spoke with her earlier on the phone to get Larry's credit card numbers. She had no idea where to look for them but finally found them. Larry kept a record of all his credit cards on a computer file but not the PINs. She gives them to the Detective when she arrives.

He asks her to describe Larry's mood as he left the office. "Larry always has a lot on his mind. He's a defense attorney. He didn't seem upset about anything, if that's what you mean."

"Did you go right home after work?"

"Yes, I have a husband and two children I must tend to."

"Can you prove you went right home?"

"Sure call my husband, ask my kids. Here's the number." Romero eliminates Debbie from his possible suspect list.

He turns to Manny and asks him the questions, even though he'd asked them before. Manny replies the same answers as before. Detectives try this tactic to trip a possible suspect up. They might inadvertently give a slightly different answer when the questions are repeated.

"Okay Ricky, it's your turn. When you arrived at the Polo Lounge, where did you park?"

"I backed into the space directly in front of the Cabaret door."

"What time was that?"

"Like I told you before, it was about 5:30pm."

"Then what did you do?"

"I opened the back door of my van, took out the accordion and a bag full of miscellaneous wires and cords for my gear. I locked the van and then walked into the main entrance of the Polo Lounge carrying those two items. As I walked in, I saw Manny and four or five Polo regulars sitting at the bar. I said hi to Sam and then went into the cabaret side to set up."

"Please continue."

"Okay, I then opened the front door of the cabaret side so I could load in the heavier gear. I don't like to carry that stuff through the bar area. It's heavy enough without making the trip longer. I went outside, once again unlocked the van and unloaded a heavy bag that I put the heavy hardware in. You know, mic stands and heavy stuff. I propped the cabaret door open with one of the outside smoker's chairs and brought in more equipment. After everything was inside, I went back outside and moved my van. Sam likes to keep the front parking spaces available to the paying customers."

Romero asks "Before you moved your van, did you close the cabaret door.

"No, I like to re-enter the Polo through the same door so I can get right to setting up the stage. It just saves time."

Aha, Romero muses. There could have been a window of opportunity for one or two people to enter that door as Ricky was moving the van to another parking space. "How long do you think it took you to move your van?"

"Well, the parking lot was starting to fill up and I drove around trying to find a close space. I'd say it took two or three minutes, at most."

"Do you always follow the same routine?"

"Yes."

"And you say this was around 5:30pm?"

"Yes, thereabouts."

"I see," said Romero.

Romero continues, "Did you see anyone enter the room through the cabaret door"

"Not while I was there, no. Once I re-entered after changing parking spaces, I moved the outside chair that was propping the door open and closed the door. I don't like to leave it open any longer than need be. It gets cold in there, real fast."

"Was there anyone else in that side of the room while you were setting up?"

"No, just me."

"Did anyone come in and then leave during this time?"

"No, they pretty much stay out of my way when I'm setting up. It's not very interesting to them. They usually just stay in the bar side and listen to the rock music on the juke box." "Do you remember what songs were playing?"

"I think "Layla," by Eric Clapton, was playing. It's a pretty long song."

"How loud was it playing?"

"Well, Manny likes to really feel the music. It's his money and Sam gives him access to the remote volume control. I guess you can say it was pretty loud."

Romero asks to hear the song. He wants to hear it at the same volume as it was played the night before. He also wants to time it. Manny plays the tune. While the song is playing, Detective Romero walks from room to room and up the stairs where the body was found. He makes mental notes of the levels in each room. He then looks at his stop watch. The song is still going on. It's now almost five minutes since it started. "Was that the song that was playing when you first came in?"

"I have to think. No, it was probably after I went out to the van. It was playing when I came back in."

"Ricky, while setting up, did you ever leave the area to go to the men's room?"

"I can't remember, maybe."

"Could it be possible that a couple of folks could have gone up those stairs while you were outside or in the men's room?"

"I suppose so."

Romero stops to think. Although there is a possibility that people could have entered while Ricky was re-parking his van, it's not likely that actually happened. The killer would have to have shot Larry immediately and then make a getaway in less than three minutes. More than likely they entered through the rear door of the cabaret side and were up there and gone before Ricky ever got there. After all, the coroner estimated the time of death to be as much as ten hours before the body was found.

That gives the killer or killers plenty of time to get out of town.

Chapter 8

Denny, the radio guy, enjoyed the dinner at the Portofino with Sam but felt tired and had a lot on his mind. He couldn't really enjoy the evening like he would have liked.

He thinks of the circumstances that brought him to this dire state. He lost his job as a TV weatherman a few months ago and is now scuffling, selling radio ads for a station in Reno. It's hard work and doesn't pay much. He prefers the high life and loves big time money. He may now be in big time trouble.

Two weeks prior, Denny had met a couple at the bar in another downtown casino. He had been gambling and needed a drink. The couple had just gotten off their shifts at the hotel. A well-dressed gentleman joined them at the bar. Denny recognized the man to be Larry Dee, a prominent defense attorney. Denny had seen and met Larry before at the Polo Lounge. Larry said hi to Denny, asked the obligatory "How are you, how's the TV business?"

Denny replied, "Don't ask, Larry. What brings you to this bar? I thought you played in the high limit section."

"Oh, my wife is over there playing the dollar slots and I decided to come over and get a drink. I can smoke here and she's in that non-smoking area." He proceeded to light up a very small custom cigar, sort of like one of those old Tiparillos. He then inserted a hundred dollar bill in the quarter poker machine.

He went through the first hundred pretty fast, as he played maximum credits each spin. He then took out another hundred and put it in. He glanced at his Rolex and grimaced. It was getting late and he had to be in court at eight in the morning. He won a few hands at the poker machine and cashed out, leaving the bartender a ten dollar toke. He then took out his iPhone and called his wife in the other part of the casino. He said goodbye to Denny and left the bar. On the way to his wife, Ruthie, he cashed the slot voucher at the cashier's cage.

Denny didn't have to get up early so he decided to have one more drink. He had enough to buy the couple a drink as well. He figured, "What the hell, it's only money. Besides, if I want another one, they'll probably reciprocate and buy me one."

They started a general social conversation, inquiring where each other is from, what they did for a living, idle conversation.

"Where are you folks from, originally?"

"Vanessa is from Indianapolis and I'm from Amarillo. We met here at the casino, through work. I'm Walt, a daytime casino bartender; Vanessa is a coffee shop food server."

Walt is a man who looks like he's been around the block a few times. He has that kind of abused alcoholic look. He looks like he's never had a solvent day in his life. He's about six feet and around 190 pounds

Vanessa appears to be small and frail, about five feet three.   She wears her strawberry blonde hair in an outdated shag style. She has sort of a "trailer trash" look. However, she could be considered "foxy" to some guys.

They appear to be romantically attached, but do not display their affection outwardly.

"Nice to meet you folks."

"How about you?"

"Well, I guess you could say I'm an under-employed media guy. I've done everything from TV work to radio sales. Right now, I'm kind of struggling, with this recession and all. It's been a little rough."

"Yeah, we're struggling too. We barely make enough to eat, let alone play these stupid machines. However, we do like to play them and they give us a free drink, now and then. Would you care for another one?"

"Why thank you." The bartender serves them and they clink glasses.

"Who was that guy you were talking to?"

"His name is Larry Dee, he's a defense attorney, here in Reno."

"He must be rich. Did you see that suit he was wearing and that Rolex?"

"Yeah, Larry's got a few bucks." "He's worked hard for his money. He's very successful."

"What's his name again?"

"Larry Dee. If you ever need a defense attorney, he's the guy to call."

Denny was getting a little tired and decided to say goodnight to the couple. He leaves for the parking garage and drives home, a little bit buzzed.

The couple leave shortly thereafter.

Three nights later, Denny is at the same bar and the couple, once again, show up.

"Hey, you two, what's happening?"

"Same old, same old. Just a different day. How 'bout you?"

"I'm only down about twenty, so far. Let me buy you guys a drink."

"Okay, thanks."

Walt asks, "Say, Denny, do you happen to know where Larry's Dee's office is?"

Denny replies, "I think it's in the Old Southwest part of town, somewhere on California Avenue. Why; do you need an attorney?"

"Maybe."

"Well, just look up the number in the phone book. I'm sure he's listed."

"Yeah, we'll do that in the morning. Next drink is on us."

Denny leaves to go to the men's room. While he's away Walt and Vanessa refine their plan. When he comes back, there's a fresh vodka rocks waiting for him.

Walt says, "The other night you were alluding to the fact that you were a little poor, these days."

"Well, I'm not going to lie to you; I am."

"Well, we've been thinking a lot, the past couple of days. Your friend, Larry Dee, seems to carry a lot of cash around with him"

"Where's this going," thinks Denny?

"We just might have a way for us all to make a little money."

"You know, I don't really know you folks. This is starting to sound a little weird."

"Relax, Denny, it's not like we're going to knock him off."

"If I wasn't so fucking broke I'd walk away from this conversation right now. However I am fucking broke, so what do you have in mind?"

"Suppose we do a simple little robbery?"

"You have got to be kidding. I could call the cops on you, right now, just for saying that."

"We don't think so. We did a little checking on you. You have unpaid markers at just about every property in this town. They're calling you every day, demanding money. I've heard, through the grapevine, they have even threatened you. You need money, big time."

"Well, you've got me there."

"Just what is your plan?"

"We need to surprise this guy. We want you to follow him around and tell us of your findings. We'll give you fifty grand for helping us. We need to know where you think he'll be on the afternoon of February 4th."

"Fifty grand?"

"That's right."

"Why February 4th?"

"We have flight reservations to Cancun on Thursday, the 5th, leaving from Salt Lake City.

"Jesus Christ, what the fuck are you thinking? What are you going to do to this guy?"

"Don't you worry about that. You just do what we ask and you'll sleep better the night of the 4th. You'll then have enough money to pay your bills and casino markers."

"I've got to think this over."

"Okay but hurry up the thought process. Here's my cell number. Call me tomorrow. If I don't answer, it's because I'm working. I'll call you back on my break,"

"I don't understand why you need me in this caper?"

"We must keep working during our regular day shifts. We have to sustain ourselves until this happens. Your time is much more flexible."

How did this happen? Denny is questioning his own sanity. If he didn't need the money so damned bad, he would have turned these low lives into hotel security. They would be behind bars and he would be on with his life. Instead, he is involved to the max. Oh well, he tells himself, "All they're asking is that he let them know where Larry is on February 4th. At least they're not getting me involved in the robbery, itself."

He is also wondering if these clowns have a criminal record. If they do, how did they get jobs at the casino? A lot of questions. "Oh well, this will give me fifty thousand dollars and I can get some sleep," he thinks. This could get some casino toughies off his back and give him a few bucks left over for dinners and drinks.

He has a feeling they haven't told him everything.

Chapter 9

Early Thursday morning, in the parking lot of the casino in Wendover, Walt and Vanessa climb into the Lexus. After the murder, they had returned to the Polo parking lot and put the Buick plates on the car; Texas plates. The cops would be looking for a Lexus with Nevada plates. They discarded the Lexus plates in a Winnemucca gas station dumpster. The iPhone on the seat is still there. They must get rid of it. They can't really use it because the authorities could find them by triangulation. They don't know the PIN so they can't check any messages. They decide they'll throw it out when they reach the salt flats.

The ATM and credit cards have worked so far. The cops couldn't possibly have the credit card numbers by now. They use the "Credit" button at the gas pumps and restaurants instead of "Debit" so they don't have to enter a PIN. No one has asked them for ID. They have about nine hundred in cash left on them.

Walt's wearing the Rolex and loving it. He's never felt this kind of luxury before. They need to get some cash somehow. They can't use an ATM. They know that will be impossible if they don't have his PIN. They know there are some big bucks in the account. They needed the money to make a fresh start in Mexico. They decide that, once they get to Salt Lake City, in the morning, they will sell the Lexus at a chop shop Walt has knowledge of and they'll pawn the Rolex. They will take a cab to the airport. They must be careful as they know the cards will soon be cancelled.

"Damn, how did this go so wrong? Why did he put up such a fight? After all, we told him we had his niece. He didn't know that it was a lie. It would've been so much better for all if he would have cooperated."

"Yeah, this worked out great," Vanessa utters, sarcastically. "You're a real fucking genius."

"Shut the fuck up, you bitch. You're the one that thought of it in the beginning."

"Don't you think by now, they're already looking for us?"

"Only if they've found the body. Remember, Denny said no one goes up to that room for days at a time. It won't start to smell for a couple of days. By then, we'll be in Mexico."

Chapter 10

The plan was working to perfection for a while. A couple days prior, Denny and Sam were talking about Larry holding a professional function at the Polo for some of his attorney buddies. Sam had mentioned that Larry was coming down to talk to him Wednesday, the 4th. Denny relayed this info to Walt and Vanessa. Denny parked across the street from Larry's office and called them when he saw Larry get into his Lexus and leave at 4:30.

They got off work at four, clocked out and waited in their car, a 1993 Buick Regal, for Denny's call. When they got the call, they hurried, but did not break any speed limits, and arrived at the Polo Lounge parking area about 4:40pm.

Within five minutes a gold Lexus sedan enters the parking lot. They immediately spot it from their vantage point. They step on the gas and pull into the space right next to Larry's car, allowing him no room to open the driver's door. He's somewhat trapped. He looks at them, and recognizes them as the couple he'd met a couple of weeks ago with Denny. He reacts like "What the fuck are you doing?"

By that time, Walt is out of his car and Vanessa has slid over so she can get out the driver's side, as well. Walt jumps in the passenger side of the Lexus and grabs Larry's iPhone. Larry picked it up as soon as he realized there was trouble. He was about to call 911. Vanessa hops in the back seat of the Lexus and puts a 38 revolver to Larry's head.

Walt says, "Don't do anything stupid. We don't want to hurt you. Just take us to your bank and make a large withdrawal, let's say two hundred thousand dollars. We want you to go to the drive-up window, ask them for a counter check and make it out for 200K, in cash. If you make a dumb move and alert them to anything, we have your teenage niece nearby. If you screw up, she gets hurt."

"Fuck you," says Larry. "Who the fuck do you think you're dealing with?"

"We know who the fuck we're dealing with; that's why you have a gun stuck in the back of your head."

Larry immediately raises his right arm and knocks the gun out of Vanessa's hand. It lands on the floor in the back. Walt grabs Larry and they wrestle violently. Vanessa finds the gun and leans over the seat back. Walt grabs the gun with a free hand and fires it, striking Larry in the chest.

This all takes place in the middle of the parking lot, an area that can hold over two hundred cars. Walt and Vanessa freeze, thinking that any second someone will be running out of one of the business to see what happened. However, they are in luck. The sports club is a few hundred feet away and it's so noisy in there and airplane could crash and no one would hear it. The Portofino isn't open yet and no one is there. They are basically in the center of the lot with no one around. The Polo lounge is about fifty feet away.

To their relief, no one comes running out. Now what the fuck do they do? They have a wounded man in a Lexus. He's been shot in the chest and is most likely dead or dying fast.

What to do? They have no chance of getting any money now. They call Denny.

"Hello."

"We've got a problem. Larry was shot and he may be dead. It just happened. It wasn't supposed to go that way."

"What?" Denny is dumbfounded. "What are you telling me? You shot Larry Dee?"

"Like I said, it was an accident. We got into a fight."

Screaming into the phone he says. "I put my faith in you two scumbags and now you fuck the whole thing up? Where are you now?

"In the parking lot, in the Lexus. There's blood all over the place."

"What the hell do you expect me to do?"

"Get your ass down here or we'll tell the cops all about it. You're as involved in this as we are."

"Fuck," I'll be right there.

Denny stops at his apartment, a couple of blocks away, and grabs three large towels. He races down to the parking lot. He sees the Lexus and goes over to it. He sees Vanessa in the back seat, in a state of shock and Walt in the front passenger seat, next to Larry's body.

"You cocksuckers, you motherfuckers, why?"

"Just Shut up. What should we do? Someone's gonna find out about this soon. We have to get rid of this body so we can delay the cops. If they find the body here, they'll figure it out real fast. We've gotta have time to get out of here. Remember, you're in this too."

"Fuck." It's now 4:55 and Denny must think fast.

"Drive the Lexus around to the back of the Polo Lounge, in the alley. I'll meet you there."

They slide Larry over and Walt takes the wheel. He backs out of the parking space and heads for the alley. Denny walks into the front door of the Polo and gives Sam a wave. He makes like he's going to the men's room in the rear but instead walks out the back door. Once he's in the alley, he spots the Lexus pulling up. They put the car in Park and Walt, a large man, drags Larry's body out. Walt assumes that they are going to throw the body in the dumpster. That would be too obvious. Denny has other plans.

"We're gonna put these towels around the wounds and take him into the Polo. No one will see us because we'll use this back door on the cabaret side. There's a loft in there above the stage. No one goes up there for days. That'll give you guys time to get out of here. Hurry, Ricky B. will be coming soon to set up his shit. Take him upstairs and lay him on the couch. They probably won't associate me with you assholes. As soon as you're finished, leave through that same door and get the fuck out of here."

Denny opens the back door for them, on the cabaret side, and then goes to the rear entrance of the bar side and reenters the lounge. Sam just assumes he came back from the men's room.   He draws Sam down to the front end so he won't see Walt carry Larry over his shoulder and up the stairs, on the cabaret side. "How's it going today, Sam?" "Okay, just waiting for the regulars to show up. Wanta have dinner tonight?"

"Yeah, maybe so."

Sam is now facing Denny at the front end of the bar and doesn't see Walt and Vanessa enter the cabaret and carry Larry up the stairs. They make sure no blood is leaking from the body by wrapping the wound with the three towels Denny gave them. They lay the body on the couch and go back down the stairs. Denny glances at the archway and sees them leave, bloody towels in hand. Because the juke box is playing, no one hears a thing.

Walt and Vanessa literally run out the door and get in the Lexus. They pull out at 5:15pm, just as Manny and his pickup enter the alley to park in the back of the Polo. He doesn't see them. That's good because he would have recognized the car. They then drive to a do-it-yourself carwash and hose the car down. They try to get as much blood off the upholstery and carpet as they can. Because the seats are leather, it makes the job a little easier. They dump the gun in a trash can at the carwash. After leaving, they spot a dumpster down the street and throw the bloody towels in it. With the aid of water and paper towels at the car wash, they have managed to clean themselves up pretty well.

While waiting for Denny to show up in the parking lot, Walt was doing what any low-life thief would do. He was removing the Rolex from Larry's left wrist and taking his wallet out of the Navy blue suit jacket pocket. He helped himself to the iPhone, as well, and then turned it off.

They make another trip to the Polo to switch plates with the Buick. They stop at their motel room to shower and change into clean clothes. They hit the road at 8:30pm, Wednesday night.

Chapter 11

Denny is trying his very best to act cool and calm in Sam's presence. In walks Manny and he greets Denny. Denny says, "I was just leaving." He finishes his drink, leaves and says to Sam, "I'll see you at the Portofino at seven."

He goes home. It's now about five thirty and Denny has an hour and a half before his dinner with Sam. He decides to take a shower. Maybe that will calm him down.

He is thinking "How did this thing get this fucked up?" He was supposed to have fifty grand in his pocket by this time. Now he's sure to be implicated in this botched robbery turned murder debacle. The casino thugs will be threatening him big-time this week. This is serious. He is standing in the shower shaking with trepidation.

"I hope those fucking idiots are far out of town," he says to himself.

He exits the shower, dries himself off, and puts on a fresh shirt, nice black slacks, and a sweater. He heads for the Portofino.

His head spinning, he's not really paying attention to his driving skills. He hears a siren and sees a cop car with its lights flashing in his rear view mirror. "Shit."

He powers down the window and waits for the officer to approach. "Good evening officer," he says.

"May I see your license and registration, please?"

"Just a sec, I have to get it out." He fumbles through the glove box and finds the registration. He pulls his license from his wallet. He gives both items to the police officer.

"Do you have proof of insurance?"

"Yes, here it is."

"Sir, I pulled you over because your headlights were not turned on. Did you not notice? I followed you for over a mile, thinking you would probably realize it and turn them on."

"Oh my God," says Denny. "I've got so much on my mind with work and all. I just didn't realize it. I'm sorry."

"Okay, I'm going to let you off with a warning. As you can see, it's dark. Be more careful."

"Okay, thank you sir."

"Boy, that was close," he thinks.

He turns into the lot and parks in front of the Portofino.

"Hey Denny, nice to see you," says Mike the Portofino bartender. Where the hell you been the last few weeks?"

"Oh, just working, you know. I'm supposed to meet Sam here in a few minutes for dinner."

Mike wonders why Denny seems to be sweating. The night air is cold and he just came in.

"Do you want your usual?"

"Please, make it a double."

In walks Sam. "God, it's cold," he says. He sees Denny at the bar and says, "Hey, let's eat, I'm starved."

The hostess seats them in a nice booth.

Sam asks, "Is everything okay?"

"Oh yeah, I just need to make a few sales. You need any radio play? Advertising always helps, you know."

"I don't know; the place does pretty well without it. I just run that one TV ad on Fox News in the morning. That seems to work."

"Well, please consider this. A lot of folks listen to the radio on their way home from work. I could put a killer package together for you."

"Well, let me give it some thought. Let's order."

"What sounds good to you", Sam asks?

"I think I'll have some pasta and a salad."

Sam says, "Just a salad for me."

They spend an hour talking about general things and Sam tells Denny he has to go back to the Polo Lounge to check on things. They both say goodbye to Mike as they leave. Outside the restaurant, Denny says, "I'll see you later."

"What, you don't want to come back to the Polo for a nightcap? I'm buying"

"Nah, I'm kind of tired. I think I'll go home and watch some TV."

"Okay, see you later."

Sam enters the Polo to see the joint jumping.

At 9:30pm he, like everyone else, hears a shot ring out in the back alley.

Chapter 12

It is now about midnight on Thursday and Detective A.J. Romero is finishing up his second interview with everyone. He knows a few things now.

The Reno crime lab has determined the bullet found in Larry came from a 38 revolver. He has learned that a 38 caliber pistol was found. The Lexus is missing. Daytime investigators have found a dilapidated 1993 Buick Regal in the parking lot with the plates missing. They are processing that car for fingerprints.

He has called Larry's cell many times now. It is obviously turned off. Thanks to Debbie, he has phoned in the credit card numbers and the cards have been cancelled. If the perpetrators try to use them, they will be declined. All merchants are alerted to call police.

Larry Dee's private investigator, Manny, is wondering about a lot of things. In his years of investigations, he has never seen anything like this. His boss has been robbed and murdered, his body found upstairs. No one had seen him enter the Polo and go upstairs. And that shot that was heard out back at 9:30 last night. What was that all about?

He asks Romero if he can leave and is given the okay. He walks out back to his truck and decides to do a little investigating on his own. He turns his headlights on and backs out of the space. He swings the truck around and proceeds slowly down the alley. After going about fifteen feet, he suddenly startled by a three dogs. They look like they've been fighting over something. He stops, gets out and the dogs growl menacingly at him. He picks up a rock and throws it at them. They disperse. He reopens the door and grabs his gun from under the seat. He turns his flashlight on and cautiously looks to find what the stir is all about. What he finds shocks him.

Between two vacant buildings behind the Polo Lounge lies a body of a large man. A large caliber pistol lies next to him. It appears that he's been shot in the left temple. Half of his head is missing. It appears to be a suicide. Manny thinks he recognizes the man. Although the face is pretty much destroyed, he can tell that it's Denny, the radio guy.

He runs back into the Polo Lounge and says to Romero, "Fuck, we've got another body. It's Denny, the radio guy."

Romero says, "Everybody wait here, don't leave."

Romero and Manny leave for the alley. Romero calls it in to Reno PD. They send two squad cars and more detectives. The coroner is called. He roughly calculates the time of death to be in the evening of February 4th. That would coincide with the gunshot everyone in the Polo Lounge heard.

Why wasn't the body found when the original police officers responded Wednesday night?

Where Manny found the body was between two vacant buildings. The body could not have been seen at night with just flashlights. The police would have had to spend much more time than they did, that night. The only reason Manny found it was because of the dogs.

Romero goes inside and informs everyone that at least one mystery may have been solved. Everyone is stunned. He asks Sam, "Who is this Denny guy?

"He's a customer that comes in here maybe once or twice a week. He's well liked. I had dinner with him yesterday at the Portofino. I can't believe it, I'm in shock."

Romero asks, "Did he seem alright at dinner?"

"Well, he was a little stressed out and tired from work. I know he's been having some financial problems."

"When is the last time you saw him?"

"When we left the restaurant, about eight o'clock."

"Did he plan to go home?"

"Yeah, he told me he was tired and wanted to go home and watch a little TV."

"Do you know where he lives?"

"A couple blocks away, in an apartment over by Virginia Lake, I think."

Romero says, "We'll check it out. You all can go home now. If I need to talk to you more, I have all your numbers and I'll call you. Please stay in the Reno area for the next few days."

Romero uses his vast detective skills and zeros in on Denny's apartment address. It is now about six in the morning and his shift is over at eight. He has a couple of hours left so he heads over to the address with two cops. At apartment 1432 he knocks on the door. No answer. He knocks again. No answer. He tries the door handle with his rubber gloved hand and is surprised to find it unlocked. The three men enter, guns drawn. There is a light on in the kitchen. The rest of the place is dark. They cautiously enter each room and find no one. The place is empty. Romero sees something on the kitchen table that appears to be a note. He picks it up and reads.

"To my family and friends, I have tried my best to be a good and honest person in my life. However, this year has taken its toll on me. I am about to lose my worldly possessions as well as my mind. I got involved in a scheme to rob Larry Dee and it backfired. I only got involved so I could get enough money to pay off people I owe.

I have let my friends and family down and I can't face the consequences that I know are coming. I have decided to take my own life rather than face all of you. I just can't do it.

The police should look for two people. The man is named Walt and the woman is named Vanessa. I don't know their last names. They were employees at the Silver Canyon Casino. I believe they may be headed to Salt Lake City in Larry Dee's gold Lexus.

I am truly sorry for what I have done. Goodbye."

Okay why did he kill himself by the Polo Lounge? After leaving Sam at the Portofino, he went home and tried to watch TV. He simple could not concentrate after what happened earlier that day. Depressed, scared, and getting more despondent by the minute, he decided to write the note about nine o'clock. He then started walking around the Virginia Lake area, debating whether to do it or not. He walked around for thirty minutes, in the cold, and then lied down between two vacant buildings close to the Polo Lounge. Crazed, shaking and crying like a baby, he put the gun to his left temple and pulled the trigger.

Romero takes the note to the station and the police start tracking down a couple with a Lexus.

Chapter 13

Eight o'clock, Thursday morning.   The guy at the chop shop opens the overhead door. Walt drives the Lexus in. The guy gives Walt a thousand dollars. No contact information is exchanged. He and Vanessa then take a cab to a nearby pawnshop in Salt Lake City, where they sell the Rolex for $550. They take the waiting cab to the Salt Lake airport. After the selling spree, they now have about twenty three hundred dollars plus two airplane tickets to Cancun. Their plane is due to leave at 11:20 am with a connection in Phoenix at 4:10 pm. They will most likely stay in a cheap motel in Cancun that evening.

What they don't know is that late Wednesday night, after the murder of Larry Dee, the night cleanup man at the carwash, in Reno, was emptying the trash cans into a larger dumpster. Most of the trash is paper towels, so when he heard the clunk of a heavy object he looked in the dumpster. He saw a gun and called police.

While Romero is home sleeping, RPD confirms a match with the found revolver and the bullet that was removed from the body. They do a search for the gun owner. The gun turns out to be registered to Alva Morrison, a lady from Amarillo, Texas. She reported it stolen a month earlier.

RPD then checks with Amarillo PD to see if anyone knows anything on two people named Walt and Vanessa. They also check with Human Resources at The Silver Canyon Hotel. The hotel comes back with Walter Ubrick and Vanessa Chalmers. Walt is from Amarillo and Vanessa has an Indianapolis address.   They follow up on every iota of information and find that the two have been in town about three weeks. Walt is 62 years of age; Vanessa 51. They were hired within two days of each other. They both lied about their criminal background and entered "None" to previous arrests.

Amarillo has a warrant out for Walter Ubrick for failure to show, in court, on a DUI charge. He also has a fairly large rap sheet with arrests for auto and jewelry theft. The department has also found that Vanessa Chalmers has been run in several times for running an illegal brothel in Indiana.

Salt Lake City has been alerted to watch for a gold Lexus with the Texas plates that were taken off the Buick in the Polo parking lot. The Salt Lake police alert the pawn shops to be on the lookout for a Rolex.

Thursday morning, after visiting the chop shop and pawn shop, Walt and Vanessa take their cab to the airport and check in without bags. "No bags," says the ticket agent?

"No, we're going on a vacation and we'll buy anything we need in Cancun."

"Okay, I'll need to see some picture ID, please."

They both produce forged passports.

"Thank you very much. Here are your boarding passes."

"Thank you."

They approach the TSA agent at the security line and show their passports and boarding passes. The agent scans them with eye piece and lets them through. The passports are damned good forgeries. They know they will not be asked for them again in Phoenix. Perhaps in Mexico.

Chapter 14

Friday morning the Reno Police Department is receiving more and more information on the travels of Walt and Vanessa. They have learned, through their investigation, the couple flew out of Salt Lake City late Thursday morning and connected with a flight in Phoenix that afternoon to Cancun. The Salt Lake police learned that a Rolex was pawned at a downtown shop. Yellow Cab has confirmed it picked up two passengers at a body shop in the industrial area of the city and then drove them downtown to a pawn shop. After that, the same cab took them to the airport.

The local police raid the body shop and discover the Lexus. They arrest the owner as his workers are trying to alter the VIN. They then recover the Rolex at the pawn shop. They confirm that it is Larry's. Ruthie is now out of the hospital. She has lists of all their personal property with serial numbers. The Rolex is definitely Larry's, as is the Lexus.

The fingerprints come back from the 38 revolver and they are identified as Walt's. Vanessa's are also on the gun. Nevada State troopers report they have discovered the Lexus plates in Winnemucca. A smashed iPhone is discovered on the shoulder of I-80 East, just outside Salt Lake City.

The detectives have received photos of the couple from the Silver Canyon Casino Human Resources and have forwarded them to the Mexican authorities in Cancun. They are advised to be on the lookout for Walter Ubrick and Vanessa Chalmers.

Chapter 15

Walt and Vanessa arise Friday morning to a sunny, beautiful day in Cancun. They can't really see the ocean from their room; it's not exactly the "Four Seasons" where they are staying. They must go find a store and buy some clothes. They only have the clothes that they left Reno in. They purchased some toiletries at the airport in Phoenix yesterday afternoon so they can at least brush their teeth and comb their hair. The motel has shampoo.

They paid cash for the items at the airport. They had dumped the wallet with the credit cards in a trash can in front of the airport. Too risky to use them now.

They only rented the motel room for one night. They must think this through today. They need a place to live and hide out.

They are pretty sure they are somewhat in the clear. It's now Friday Morning. The body will probably be found today or tomorrow. After then, it will surely start to smell and alert even a drunk at the bar. They know that Denny is not about to blab. He certainly doesn't want to be implicated in this fiasco.

Of course, they do not know that Larry Dee's body was discovered Wednesday night and their accomplice, Denny, committed suicide that same night, leaving a note naming them as the perpetrators.

They also do not know that a gun was found with their fingerprints and that Detective A.J. Romero and Reno PD are hot on their trail.

They leave to exchange some money into Pesos, get some breakfast, and also do a little clothes shopping. They have never been to Mexico before, even though Walt is from Amarillo. They have no idea what a Peso is worth or how to order anything in a restaurant. They have heard, however, that the larger tourist hotels are American friendly and the hotel staffs usually speak English.

Because they are now walking, their first stop is at a nearby bank. They tell the teller that they would like to exchange three one hundred dollar bills for Mexican money. The teller understands and gives them 3000 Pesos.

They walk to a tourist hotel on the beach. It's a beautiful place with chandeliers and plush carpeting. Valets are parking luxury cars and a doorman opens the hotel entrance door for them. "Gracias," Walt says. Vanessa gives him a sneer.

They find the hotel coffee shop and order from pictures. The waiter recognizes their plight and asks them in English what they would like.

"Scrambled eggs and bacon for both of us, please"

They finish their breakfast and ask the waiter how much the tab is, in Pesos.

He tells them and they leave the money in the folder the waiter leaves on the table. They exit the restaurant, paranoid that some cop will jump out of the woodwork and nail them.

They walk out of the lobby into the driveway area. To their dismay, there is a Cancun police car parked in the driveway but no one is behind the wheel. In an instant, another cop car pulls up. The cop gets out, looks at a sheet of paper and looks around. He spots Walt and Vanessa on the steps and speaks into his shoulder radio.

Walter is suspicious. He thinks they might be on to them. He grabs Vanessa and heads back inside. Almost running, he leads her to an exit sign. They go through the door and see stairs going up and down. Without time to think, they head upstairs. "How did they find us? How did they know we're here? Vanessa doesn't answer. She's trying to climb stairs.

"Could that waiter have called the police? Maybe there's an alert on us"

"Shut up and move," Vanessa says.

They get to the third floor and hear footsteps from below. "Shit, they know we're in the stairs," Walt says. They leave the stairway on the fourth floor and enter a hotel hallway. In the hallway is a maid's service cart. She is cleaning room #423.

Running now, they see that the #423 door is open and the maid is inside. Thinking fast, he shoves Vanessa inside the room and he continues down the hall, trying to convince anyone who may be watching that he is by himself, and not part of a couple.

Vanessa is shocked. How could he do this? The maid doesn't realize that Vanessa isn't the true occupant of the room so it doesn't bother her that she goes in the bathroom and locks the door. The maid goes about her business cleaning the rest of the room.

In about thirty seconds, two policias with guns drawn, run past the room. One of them abruptly stops and goes back to the maid cart. He looks in the room and just sees the maid. He catches up with his partner and they continue the search for the couple.

By now, a total of eight policia cars have arrived and there are sixteen cops running around looking for the fugitives.

Disculpe senora, Esta todo bien? The maid is asking the lady in the bathroom if everything is alright.

"Yes, I'll be right out."

Meanwhile, Walt has managed to elude his pursuers and has reentered the fourth floor. The maid's cart is still there and he enters the room. In English he asks, "Where is she?" The maid doesn't understand English but thinks he might be looking for his wife. She points to the bathroom door. He says "Vanessa, come on out, let's go." She opens the door, tears streaming down her face, and comes out. They leave the room and run down the hall to a laundry chute which he has discovered in his travels around the hallways.

It's the only way out. There are cops everywhere. She goes first. She only weighs 108. It's a forty five foot drop into a cart filled with dirty laundry. She lands in the cart filled with sheets and towels, uninjured. She quickly gets out and waits for Walt. Walt is way too large to fit into the chute. Now what? He whispers down the chute to wait for him there. He'll try another route. He hopes she's heard him.

The workers in the Laundry room are puzzled as to why this American woman has suddenly appeared. Where did she come from and why is she here? A laundry supervisor asks her, in Spanish, what she wants. "Que quieres?" Vanessa doesn't understand. She is panicky and runs out of the laundry room.

She immediately bumps into a hotel security officer. He asks this obviously American woman what she's doing, in English.

She replies, "I'm lost."

"Where is your room?"

"On the fourth floor, I think."

"Do you have the room number?"

"I forgot."

"Do you have your room entry card?"

"I lost it."

He realizes by now that something is amiss, here. He calls on his hand radio for backup and another security guard comes down.   Hotel security has also notified the Cancun police Captain on the Lobby floor. He also comes down with a paper in his hand. He looks at the APB with the Silver Canyon employee photos and realizes he's got the fugitive Vanessa Chalmers trapped. He calls for more officers.

Other police come down to the basement hallway and cuff Vanessa. She doesn't resist. She is much too small to put up any kind of fight.

They question her about the whereabouts of her partner Walter.

"I have no idea". Cockily, she says, "If you don't have him by now, he's left the building."

The Captain gets on the radio to a sergeant. "Anyh suerte, any luck?

"No senor, negativo."

Word has now gotten back to Reno PD that the couple had been spotted in a hotel coffee shop in Cancun. A hotel waiter had recognized them from a flyer that was posted in the kitchen.

As soon as Reno determined they were in flying to Cancun, they e-mailed the poster to Cancun PD. Within two hours, all the major hotels and their security details had descriptions of the couple.

It's now about ten in the morning and the Cancun police have Vanessa in their custody. They are scanning the hotel for Walter but he cannot be found. How could he have slipped out?

After Vanessa went feet first into the laundry chute, Walt looked out the window of the elevator lobby on the fourth floor. He sees a swimming pool forty feet below. He thinks perhaps he could break a window and jump into the pool. No one is using it and all he would have to do is hop over the fence to make his getaway. He could then go around back, where he presumes the the laundry area to be, and look for Vanessa.

Walt decides that jumping from that height might be too dangerous. He decides to take the stairway down to the second floor. He exits the stairway and doesn't see anyone. He goes to that floor's elevator lobby and looks out. No one in the pool, no cops in sight. He kicks the window and breaks it. As his foot and shoulder travel through the glass, he is badly cut. Bleeding, he jumps as far as he can and lands in the pool, six inches from the edge. The cops, patrolling the third floor, hear glass shattering and run to to the window to see what's going on. As they look out, they see a soaking wet, bloody figure climbing over the pool fence. They radio for backup, run down the stairs and pursue the subject on foot.

Walt doesn't realize he's been spotted and runs around the parking lot to the back of the building where he assumes the laundry area is located. He is running but his leg is in pain and the blood is leaving a very apparent trail. It is flowing from his soaking wet jeans and shirt.

He sees a utility driveway and runs down it, thinking that's where she'll be.

The cops have this thing set up. He screams her name and she comes out. He runs to her and they grab him. A struggle ensues and he manages to grab one the cop's guns. With his left hand, he yanks it out of the holster and fumbles for the trigger. Left handed, he pulls the trigger. The burly Mexican policia falls to the ground. Vanessa is screaming, "Stop it, stop it, they've got us."

Walter then takes the gun and points it at her. He realizes he's about to get shot and he can't bear the thought of her rotting in some Mexican jail. He actually cares about her. One of the cops chasing him in the driveway aims and fires. The bullet hits him in the chest and goes through the heart.

Walter drops, looking Vanessa in the eyes on the way down.

She thinks he mouths the words "I love y - -"

It's over.

Chapter 16

Anthony Joseph Romero gets a call Friday around noon. The scumbags have been captured. He is dead and she's in custody in a Mexican jail. Assuming she'll be extradited from Mexico, she will probably receive life in some isolated Northern Nevada prison.

He has learned Walter was shot thought the heart. Ironically, Larry Dee was too. Maybe this is a kind of justice.

It's his day off. He pours himself a cup of coffee and decides to go to the Polo Lounge later for a drink. He kind of likes the place.

Made in United States
North Haven, CT
15 September 2022

24145622R00030